This is an
← Alien Scale Monster in space

TOM GATES

BEST
BOOK DAY
EVER!
(so far)

By
Liz Pichon

SCHOLASTIC

First published in the UK in 2013 by Scholastic Children's Books
An imprint of Scholastic Ltd
Euston House, 24 Eversholt Street
London, NW1 1DB, UK
Registered office: Westfield Road, Southam, Warwickshire, CV47 0RA
SCHOLASTIC and associated logos are trademarks and/ or registered
trademarks of Scholastic Inc.

ISBN 978 1 407 13681 3

A CIP catalogue record for this book is available from the
British Library.

Printed by GGP Media GmbH, Germany
Papers used by Scholastic Children's Books are made from wood
grown in sustainable forests.

1 3 5 7 9 10 8 6 4 2

www.scholastic.co.uk/zone

Important Stuff

# MASSIVE!

THANKS 😊 to all the children, teachers and librarians whose costumes, which I saw on various **WORLD BOOK DAYS,** SPARKED OFF THE IDEAS FOR THIS BOOK.

LIZ PICHON xx

**10** MERITS

Hairy bug

Coming SOON!

This book has been specially written and published for
World Book Day 2013.
For further information, visit
www.worldbookday.com

World Book Day in the UK and Ireland is made possible
by generous sponsorship from National Book Tokens,
participating publishers, authors and booksellers.
Booksellers who accept the

£1 World Book Day Book Token
bear the full cost of redeeming it.

World Book Day, World Book Night and Quick Reads
are annual initiatives designed to encourage everyone
in the UK and Ireland – whatever your age – to
read more and discover the joy of books.

World Book Night is a celebration of books
and reading for adults and teens on April 23,
which sees book gifting and celebrations in
thousands of communities around the country.
www.worldbooknight.org

Quick Reads provides brilliant short new books
by bestselling authors to engage adults in reading.
www.quickreads.org.uk

GOOD stuff to know!

Look out for more TOM GATES books:

The Brilliant World of Tom Gates

Excellent Excuses (and other good stuff)

Everything's Amazing (sort of)

Genius Ideas (mostly)

and coming soon...

Tom Gates is Absolutely Fantastic (at some things)

← Scale Alert

Fool Alert

Hairy Bug Alert

Empty
Space

↑ This space is BLANK so you can
make your own book plate
(see page 84) and STICK it in.
(Don't draw on books ... page 76.)

## Oakfield School Book Week

This year the whole school (including the teachers) will take part in an exciting week of CELEBRATING BOOKS.

Don't forget to dress up as your favourite character from a book and take part in the BOOK PARADE.

There will be BIG PRIZES for the BEST costumes.

It's going to be BOOKTASTIC!

Mr Keen
Headmaster

This is EXCELLENT NEWS ...

... for LOTS of reasons,

like these:

Yeah!

3

**1.** **A**ll the teachers are far more cheerful than usual.

Mr Fullerman

la la
Mrs Nap

Yo, kids!
Mrs Worthington

**2.** **I**t's the only time you can *point* AND L**A**U**G**H at a teacher and not get into trouble.

Look at Mr Fullerman
Ha! Ha!
Ha!
Ha!

**3.** We don't do NORMAL lessons. Instead we'll do workshops and loads of other good stuff (even in maths).

Maths teacher Mrs Nap →

Let's play a game!

**4.** You get to dress up as your FAVOURITE character from a  book and maybe WIN a PRIZE.

PLUS there's the

 BIG BOOK SWAP as well.

IT'S GOING TO BE AMAZING!

When I get back home,  I tell Mum that I can't WAIT to go to school next week because it's going to be so much fun. Then she says,

> Are you feeling OK, Tom?

And puts her hand on my head like I'm sick or something. I remind Mum that it's actually

**BOOK WEEK** and give her Mr Keen's letter.

Then I ask,

> Can we make my costume NOW?

Because last year, things didn't exactly go to plan.

(This is what happened.)

I wanted to go dressed as

# THE IRON MAN

using two cardboard boxes

covered in LOTS

of foil.

It was quite late before we started
to make it and Mum said,
"This won't take long to finish."
Then she _r o l l e d_ out the foil ...
all five centimetres of it.

5cm

I said, "I think we need to buy some
more." But the shops were already s h u t.

"Don't worry, Tom," Mum assured me as I

went to bed.

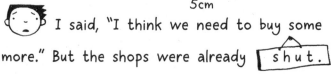

I'll think of
something.

"Something" turned out
to be Christmas wrapping paper.

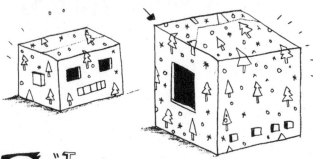

"It's covered in Christmas trees 🎄
and I can see snowflakes too!" I said.

"Not from a distance –
or if you keep moving," Mum told me,
trying to be positive. "At least it's all
SHINY and Silver.

"I'll look like a GIANT PRESENT, not
THE IRON MAN."
Mum suggested that maybe I could lose

 the head box and find something else to wear instead?

"Like what?" I wondered.

"Let me see what your father has in his shed." 

Which didn't sound that promising.

When Dad came into the kitchen, he asked, "Who's that GIANT present for?"

"It's supposed to be my IRON MAN costume."

"Oh I see," Dad said, when he obviously didn't. I told him,

"Mum's in your shed now, looking for other ideas."

Which made Dad PANIC and RUSH outside.

"Oh no!"

Left on my own and realizing I only had 🕐 twenty minutes before school, I decided that maybe I should at least try on the body part of my costume, just to ☉ ☉ see what it looked like.

Then Delia → (my grumpy teenage sister) walked in and started

LAUGHING at me ...

... A LOT.

Ha Ha Ha Ha!

I told her, "Get LOST, DELIA, I'm trying on my **BOOK WEEK** costume."

And she said,

Going dressed as an idiot, then?

(Which was annoying.)

Mum came back from the shed holding an empty biscuit tin.

"Will this do, Tom?"

I said, "No, Mum, I'm not wearing a biscuit tin on my head."

"Why not? It's an improvement," Delia added helpfully.

Dad was just pretending he didn't know where the biscuits had gone.

Yum

Wasn't me

Then he EXPERTLY 🙂 changed the subject by suggesting I could borrow his 🤠 hat instead and go dressed as the character from the *FIND FRANKIE* books. Which was a

GREAT idea, because I already had a black 👕 T-shirt and STRIPY 🧦🧦 socks.

Mum said she'd draw some glasses on me with her make-up pencil too.

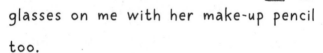

But don't rub your eyes or they'll smudge.

Considering the $\equiv\equiv$ RUSH I'd
been in, I thought I looked OK. ☺

Dad even gave me a lift to
school so I wasn't late.
The only trouble was, when I
got there ...

Dad's hat

Me dressed
as FIND FRANKIE

... I wasn't the only kid dressed up as **FRANKIE,**

**FRANKIE** was EVERYWHERE

(and not difficult to find at all).

So this year, to avoid any more book costume disasters, I'm making mine right away.

What do you want to be, then?

Mum asks.

I show her the book Granny Mavis gave me 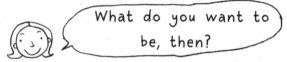 last week. I've been trying to collect the WHOLE series and this one is

← MY FAVOURITE

(so far).

"I want to be an **Alien Scale Monster**."

Mum sighs and says,

OK, I think I can manage that.

As I've already got a cardboard box and some green paint for the alien head, I make a list of everything else we need:

Mum wants me to find an OLD pair of pyjamas too. Which seems a bit ODD?

* Shiny green card for the scales

* A few extra eyes for the alien head

* Glue

* More foil – just in case

Mum assures me,

They'll be covered in scales you won't see them at all.

"**B**ut I don't have any OLD  pyjamas," I say.

**M**um says she'll find something else for me to wear when she goes into town.

"Nothing fancy as it's just for a costume."

Which is fine by me. (RESULT!)

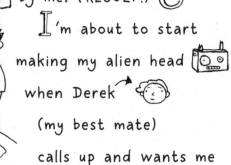 **I**'m about to start making my alien head when Derek (my best mate) calls up and wants me to come over to his house.

It's an EMERGENCY, he says.

18

As Derek only lives next door,
I'm there in a  *FLASH.*

He says, "I can't decide who to
be for **BOOK WEEK**. I need ideas or
Mum will make me go as something
embarrassing."

So I say,
"Let's have a snack
first, then we can
think of something
GREAT." Which is a good idea. ☺

While we're busy thinking
Derek's dad (Mr Fingle) comes
over to say hello and asks,

What are you boys up to, then?

Derek says, 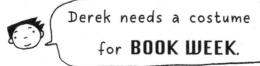 Nothing much

at exactly the same time as I say...

Derek needs a costume for **BOOK WEEK**.

Whoops.

Mr Fingle says he has LOADS of books we can use for ideas.

Which makes Derek roll his eyes and say, OK, Dad. I tell Derek that we might as well have a LOOK at them.

Like we have a choice, Derek says as Mr Fingle brings over an ENORMOUS pile of books.

Rock n Roll

Bands That Changed the World

Best MUSIC

He's already pointing out possible costumes for Derek – who's ⎡not⎤ keen on most of them. Right up until he spots a Very cool black and white photo.

 Derek says, "Now that's a good costume." I agree. ☺

Do you think it matters he's a real person and not just from a story?

Derek asks.

Mr Fingle says no one could possibly think that dressing up as Elvis was a bad idea. So that's settled.

Uh huh

Derek's going as **ELVIS** and I'm going to be an **Alien Scale Monster.**

We decide to go back to my house when Mr Fingle starts singing his favourite **ELVIS** songs.

Shame.

Back at home, Derek helps me to finish painting my alien head.

Mum comes back from town with lots of shiny green paper for the scales and **LOADS** more **EYES.**

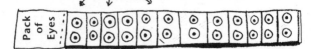

Pack of Eyes

She tells us, "It was much better value to buy them in a large pack." Derek and I stick most of the EYES on my costume.

Then the rest of the eyes, we put to VERY good use around the house ...

... in the kitchen ...

... bathroom ...

... on coats ...

... and Delia's sunglasses too.

In the morning Mum looks a bit tired. "I've been up all night attaching all your scales," she says. "I've got a few more to add but you can try the **whole** costume on `now` if you want to." Which is a good idea.  YES!

I really hope this costume will  me a {PRIZE.}
The first prize is usually a BIG  BOOK TOKEN

– which would be very handy, as I'm trying to collect `ALL` of the

ALIEN  SCALE  MONSTER  BOOKS.

And there's ONE in the series that's been impossible to find...

# Alien SCALE MONSTERS— IN SPACE.

My Granny Mavis and Granddad Bob have been looking everywhere for it as well.

Book SHOP

No

There's a rumour another **prize** is a LARGE jar of JELLY BEANS.

jelly beans

If you insist

(That would be a good win too.)

$I$ go and put on my costume.
$H$ead first...

Now the rest of
the body.
Then I carefully
do up the zip, but
one scale seems to get STUCK

- and falls off.

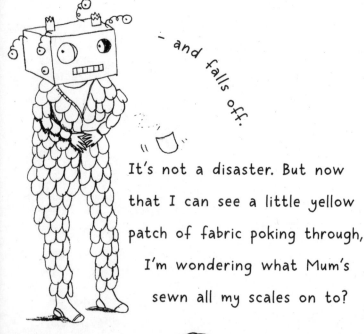

It's not a disaster. But now
that I can see a little yellow
patch of fabric poking through,
I'm wondering what Mum's
sewn all my scales on to?

Not that it matters, because I think my costume LOOKS GREAT!

Thanks, Mum

BOOK PARADE - here I COME!

(Not long to go.)

**BOOK WEEK**

at Oakfield School!

I'm being EXTRA jolly and smiley today because we have a whole week of GOOD stuff to look forward to. AND my **Alien Scale Monster** costume is looking fantastic (if I do say so myself). :)

In Class 5F, Mr Fullerman thinks we are being

**TOO NOISY.** He says,

**"I know you're all excited about this week but you need to QUIETEN DOWN a bit, please."**

But when that doesn't work, he says it again.

# "QUIETEN DOWN!"

(Which does the trick.)

Marcus Meldrew →

(who sits next to me) wants to

know "who" I'm going to be

in the BOOK PARADE.

 But when I start

to tell him he just

BUTTS in and talks RIGHT over

me, saying...

Well, MY costume is
AMAZING!

Really, Marcus ... groan.

Yes, I'll definitely win a prize
this year.

"How do you know that?" I say.

And he says, "Because I've written my

own story ... ABOUT ME."

"That sounds ... really interesting," I say - trying to sound interested.

"It is. I'm the SUPERHERO who saves the WORLD. That's who I'm coming dressed as."

And I say, "As yourself?"

Marcus gets a bit IRRITATED and says, "NO, not as ME ... as SUPER MARCUS the superhero." I say, "OH, I see."

Then I nudge AMY PORTER (who sits on the other side of me)

and tell her,

"Guess what Marcus is coming dressed as for the BOOK PARADE?"

And she says,  "What?"

And I say,

"As a SUPERMARKET."

"A SUPERMARKET?" Amy says,

and I say, "Yes, a SUPERMARKET, how funny is that?"

Marcus is getting ANNOYED.

He says, "NO, not a supermarket.

I'm SUPER MARCUS."

Then he grabs some paper and starts doing a drawing of himself as a superhero.

"SEE, like THIS," he says while muttering "idiots" to himself.

"Oh ... now we get it," I say (when really I got it all the time).

THIS is ME as a SUPER ~~HERO~~ Z

Super Marcus

While **M**r Fullerman is doing the register, I decide to add a little extra something to Marcus's picture.

Which makes Amy laugh.

The REST of **BOOK WEEK** is REALLY *fun* too.

Every day there's been EXTRA good stuff to do. So far I have:

° Taken part in Mr Sprocket's "storytelling with sounds" class.

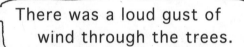

There was a loud gust of wind through the trees.

I thought my whoopee cushion

**pphhwwaaaaS**

Ha Ha

really brought the story to life. Ha

° Made recycled paper in art.

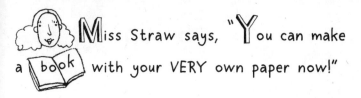 Miss Straw says, "You can make a book with your VERY own paper now!"

(Looking at what Norman Watson's done – I'm not sure that's going to happen.) 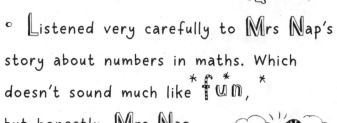 Ta dah!

° Listened very carefully to Mrs Nap's story about numbers in maths. Which doesn't sound much like *fun*, but honestly, Mrs Nap surprised us all.

° Met a REAL-life author who writes books on **MONSTERS** and other

Yuck!

EEwwwww

kinds of DISGUSTING creatures. He told us how to spell "slime" like this:

(My slug)

**S**lugs

**L**eave

**I**cky

**M**arks

**E**verywhere

Which is a good way of remembering it.

But I think the most EXCITING part of **BOOK WEEK** has been when I spotted a kid walking around school holding a copy of ALIEN SCALE MONSTERS – IN SPACE!

I've been trying to get that book for AGES! It's been OUT OF STOCK everywhere. Which was driving me BONKERS. ◌̈

Right now, I'm in the queue for lunch and I see the kid again, STILL holding that book. →

I ask Norman to

SAVE MY PLACE

so I can go and ask where he got it from. But by the time I squeeze through the crowd –

Huh?

the kid's gone.

AND to make things worse ...

# SO HAS MY PLACE IN THE LUNCH QUEUE!

...TAKEN BY MARCUS MELDREW, who's

jumped ahead and looks all SMUG and pleased with himself!

He won't let me back in, either.

Marcus says, "Bad luck, Tom. You snooze, you lose." zzzzzz

Then Mrs Worthington says I need to join the queue at the END of the line.

(Which is annoying, as I'm HUNGRY!)

rumble rumble

After lunch (which I'm still cross about), Mr Fullerman wants us to create our

**VERY OWN MONSTERS like the author did earlier.**

Mr Fullerman tells us,

**I'm looking forward to reading and seeing all your horrible creations!**

Me too. I don't have to look far for my inspiration...

# This is a SMUG MUG MONSTER.

It's very annoying and likes to BOAST about how good it is at everything (when really it's RUBBISH).

Flaky skin

Smug Mugs have nasty FLAKY skin which is a disgusting shade of green. Don't stare at Smug Mug for too long - or you'll feel SICK.

Smug Mugs say really stupid things like:

Nah nah nah nah nah...

   and

You snooze, you lose.

Good work for creating a truly revolting MONSTER, Tom! I'll be looking forward to seeing your choice of costume for the Book Parade too!
Mr Fullerman
5 Merits

**YEAH!**

The BOOK PARADE can't come soon enough for me. Because Marcus STILL won't shut up about how he's going to win a prize on FRIDAY.

My story and costume are AMAZING.

(Blah blah blah ... yawn, yawn.)

The BOOK PARADE is actually TOMORROW. I try to tell him several times, but as usual, he just keeps talking.

Instead I say, "Marcus ... you are a genius."

(He's not.)

# AT LAST, ⇨ THE BOOK PARADE
## IS TODAY!

I put my costume on – then realize I can't eat my breakfast now.

Oh –

When I take OFF the alien head, Delia pretends to be more scared of my face.

It's HIDEOUS!

"Ha ha, very funny," I say.

Derek is waiting for me outside so we can walk to school together and not look too weird.

"Excellent, Elvis," I say.

"Thanks, **Alien Scale Monster**." he says.

Elvis

In school, I can see ⊙ ⊙ a
PIRATE telling everyone to
"get to your classes or
you'll have to walk the
plank..."
It's only when I hear
loads of keys jingling
that I REALIZE it's
Caretaker Stan.

I head to my class, where Mr Fullerman
isn't at his desk yet. There's a sign on
the board that says

YOU HAVE BEEN WARNED!
SOMEONE ELSE has replaced
Mr Fullerman TODAY...

I give **AMY PORTER** a bit of a **SHOCK** when I ask her, "**W**hat's that message about?"

She says, "**AGH!**" followed by,

"Who knows ... is that you, Tom?"

"**Y**es, I'm an **Alien Scale Monster**," I say. "Where's your costume?"

**AMY** points to a **very** impressive car.

"Florence and I made it. It's Chitty Chitty Bang Bang."

"Good job, Amy," I say.

Then I ask her,

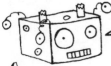

Where's Super Marcus?

Amy says, "You'll never guess what."

 "What?" I ask.

"He forgot it was the BOOK PARADE TODAY and didn't wear his costume."

(Shame.)

"I tried to tell him," I say.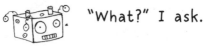

Amy says, "He called home but everyone was out, so Mrs Mumble's taken him to find a spare costume from the school dressing-up box."

"I wonder what it will be?" I say.

We don't have to wait long before Marcus comes back dressed as ...

a butterfly?

"I'm NOT a butterfly," Marcus tells us.

"A moth?" I ask.

"NO, not even close," Marcus says. Then he takes out a missing piece of costume and puts it on.

"I'm an elephant, from da *Jungle Book* ... DATS all dey ad."

(It's hard to hear what he's saying with the trunk on.)

Amy and I both tell Marcus that it's a good costume and he says,
"Tanks."

(I think he means Thanks.)

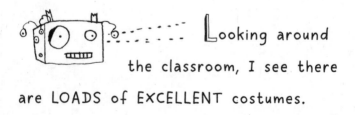 Looking around the classroom, I see there are LOADS of EXCELLENT costumes.

Solid has come as a GIANT book.
Norman is some kind of **hairy** bug?

Julia Morton is Alice from *Alice's Adventures in Wonderland*. Brad and Paul are Thing 1 and Thing 2 from *The Cat in the Hat*.
We're all still waiting for
Mr Fullerman when Amy says,

"Is this yours?" She's holding up one of my scales.

"Yes ... it is," I say.

I'm trying to stick it back on when suddenly...

49

Mr Fullerman arrives dressed as ...

THE CHILD CATCHER.

He shouts,

**Hello, children!**

Which makes some kids JUMP.

Everyone stops talking.

Mr Fullerman laughs and says,

I should dress like
this more often!

Then he tells us that Mr Keen and
Mrs Nap will be making notes on all the
costumes in our assembly to award the
PRIZES at the BOOK PARADE.
**"And this year** GREAT MANOR
SCHOOL **will be joining us for an
EVEN BIGGER** BOOK PARADE **at
the school fields!"** And the whole
class **groan**. (Because GREAT MANOR
SCHOOL always wins EVERYTHING.)
**"Don't worry, there'll be PLENTY of
PRIZES for BOTH schools,"**
Mr Fullerman says.

YEAH! We all cheer. Then I lift
up my arm ... and another scale drops off.

# A BOOK WEEK MESSAGE
## FROM MR KEEN
(our headmaster)

My class set off down the hall
for our assembly, but it's tricky
SQUEEZING everyone in
with their costumes on. I have to take
off my alien head when Mr Keen starts
talking so the kids behind me can see.

 **"Good morning,
OAKFIELD SCHOOL.
GGGGGGGRRRRRRRrrrrrrrrr!"**

We all laugh at Mr Keen's silly noise

(and his furry suit with ears).

Ha! Ha! Ha!

"Good morning, Mr Keen."

He tells us we all look

**FANTASTIC.**

Then he asks, **"Does anyone know who I am?"**

S I L E N C E .

Mr Keen does another

**GGGGRRRRRrrrrrrrrrrrrrrrrrr.**

(Like that's going to help.)

One kid puts up his hand and says, "A lion?"

**"No, not quite."** Another suggests  he's "a very angry cat?"

**"Try again."**

It's only when the other teachers join him that we can all see who they are.

Goldilocks and the three bears.

Oh yes ... so they are.

At the end of assembly, Mrs Nap and  Mr Keen look carefully at everyone's costume as they leave. They make notes on WHO'LL be the prize-winners later on.

I'm trying to do the BEST MONSTER walk I can to impress them. But as soon as I move, EVEN MORE scales fall off.

Julia Morton (who's behind me) says I look like a ( Zombie fish. )

Thanks, Julia.

Then she adds, "You're missing some scales."

I pretend that I'm not bothered at all.

It's fine.

"No one will notice,"

I say.

(Much.)

Throughout the rest of the day, my scale 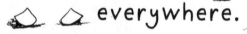 problem gets worse ...

... and worse ...

... and worse...

I'm shedding them everywhere.

Solid hands me another batch in the dinner hall.

"We could try sticking them on with tape," he says.

It's a good idea,

but there's no time and no sticky tape either.

And the bell's just gone, so everyone will be heading off for the **BOOK PARADE** at the school playing fields. Great Manor School have already arrived and are waiting for us.

I can see some VERY impressive-looking costumes too.

(Groan.)

Class by class, Oakfield School file into rows opposite the Great Manor children.

We leave a nice clear pathway

to

walk

down

for the

PARADE.

Marcus Meldrew stands next to me and says, "Your costume's a bit RUBBISH, isn't it?"

He's holding more of my scales in his hand.

So I say,

It's **not** a RUBBISH costume. At least I didn't forget mine!

Then I add...

If all the scales do eventually fall off, I'll just be an **ALIEN MONSTER** instead.

Marcus laughs and says, "**M**ore like a yellow **FLUFFY**  kitten monster."

What does he mean, YELLOW FLUFFY KITTEN MONSTER?

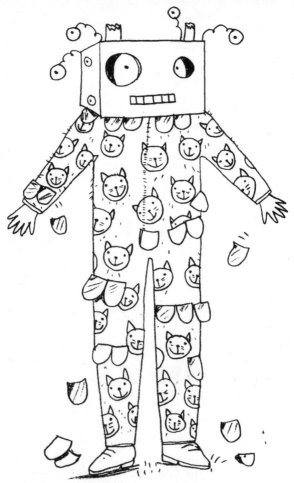

I didn't take much notice of what Mum had ~~sewn~~ - sorry, STUCK all my scales on to.

I REALLY wish I had now.

I find Derek and ask him, "Be honest, how many kittens can you see?"

"Errr, maybe one or two ... sorry, three ... no, SEVEN, eight ... actually, loads."

This is NOT good news.

I can't believe Mum used a YELLOW ALL-IN-ONE SUIT COVERED WITH FLUFFY LITTLE KITTENS!

I'm like a tree losing its leaves in the autumn. I'll have to keep my alien head on so NO ONE will see it's ME. It's VERY embarrassing.

Mr Keen and Ms Taylor

from Great Manor

welcome everyone to the

**BOOK PARADE.**

> Marvellous costumes, don't
> you agree, Mr Keen?

Ms Taylor says.

> **I do, Ms Taylor.**

They've already taken a good
LOOK at the costumes and now
they're about to read out the
names of the PRIZE-WINNERS for
both schools.

Normally I'd be VERY excited. But
wearing a yellow onesie covered in
FLUFFY kittens isn't exactly
what I had in mind for the BOOK PARADE.

Just when I think things can't get any worse,  Mr Keen points to a PHOTOGRAPHER from the local paper who'll be

**taking photos of this year's WINNERS.**

(I'm thinking, PLEASE not me ...

PLEASE don't call my name!)

The first names called out ARE:
**AMY** and Florence with their
brilliant car.

Then Solid's called next (there goes my
hiding place). Then some kid from Great
Manor in a cool scary costume.

There are more children from both
schools – including Norman Watson,

who's LEAPING around.

I'm beginning to think I'm SAFE ...

when I hear Ms Taylor say,

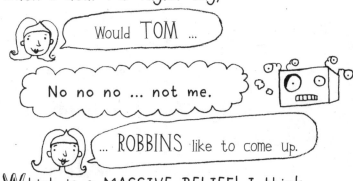

Would TOM ...

No no no ... not me.

... ROBBINS like to come up.

Which is a MASSIVE RELIEF! I think
I've avoided TOTAL humiliation.

Phew

Finally I begin to *relax* (a bit).
I unfold

my arms and watch as the very last scale falls off.

Then Mr Keen says,

"And LAST BUT NOT
LEAST ... Tom Gates
dressed as an

Alien Scale Monster!"

# HUH!
# OH NO!

Mr Fullerman can tell I'm [not] keen to join the parade.

"I've lost all my scales, sir," I say.

**Off you go, Tom!**

he says,

as the photographer *moves* all the

winners into a line. I can hear some kids

whispering ( Why the kittens? )

So I try hiding behind Solid

(again).

I am a
GIANT
BOOK
By Solomon
Stewart

The photographer says, "Everyone look at me and say BOOK PARADE!"

Norman Watson gets a bit over EXCITED and does a MASSIVE JUMP, trying to get into the photo.

He pushes me and I knock into Solid, who loses his balance and topples into another couple of kids.

They *fall* over and EVERYONE in the line is left "WOBBLING" around.

 Amy and Florence just  manage to get out of the way so their car is safe.

The teachers *rush* over to check everyone's OK (they are).

Somehow I've managed to LAND BANG SMACK...

into a slightly SOGGY patch of MUD.

But while I'm down on the ground, I suddenly get an  IDEA.

I need to make the **most** of this MUDDY situation and get EVEN GRUBBIER.

I do a few angel-wing moves, then a lot of quick *ROLLING* around in the mud, which does the trick.

I grab a few more handfuls of mud before the photographer is ready to try again for the photo. Only this time, I'll be an **ALIEN SWAMP MONSTER**. (Which is fine by me!) When the photographer says "SMILE!" I'm happy to WAVE.

mud

mud

Then I pick up my **PRIZE**.
HOPEFULLY, NOW
I can get a copy of
**Alien Scale Monsters –
in SPACE.**

Which would be AMAZING.

When I get home, it takes
a while to explain what exactly
happened to my costume.

Mum says
she won't use glue on
fluffy fabric again.

"At least you won a prize,
Tom," she says. (Which is
true.) Turns out the BIG JAR OF
BEANS PRIZE was just a
rumour after all.

(Shame.)

# THE LAST DAY
## OF BOOK WEEK

Is TODAY.

(I'm very glad I don't have to wear my costume again, as it's still a bit SOGGY.) I've found a few (OLD) alien books for the

BIG BOOK SWAP

after school too, which I mustn't forget to bring.

In class, everyone has brought books to swap as well. I'm looking at AMY's books while Marcus keeps going ON and ON and ON about his costume.

Blah
Blah
Blah

He says...  "I would have won a PRIZE if I'd remembered to bring it." (Really ... groan.) Marcus is driving me NuTS,

NOTES:

so I get out my sketchbook and draw this doodle. Which helps me to IGNORE him ... for a while.

Marcus interrupts my drawing. He's NUDGING me. WHAT NOW?
He says, "That's my book you're drawing on."

And I say, "No it's NOT."

And he says, "Yes, it is MY book actually."

I say, "THIS is MY book ... oh it's yours." I tell Marcus I'm sorry, but he's already put his hand up.

Tom Gates has just drawn on my book, sir.

(Groan.)

Mr Fullerman comes over to see what's going on. **"Did you draw in Marcus's book, Tom?"**

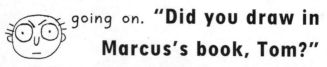

"Yes, sir, by accident - I thought it was mine!"

He says I shouldn't be drawing in ANY books. "Yes, sir." Marcus says, "I wanted to swap this book - who'll want it now?"

(That will be me, then.) I swap my **Alien Scale Monster** book for a book on bugs. THE BIG BOOK OF BUGS

Mr Fullerman thinks it's a very good solution. Then he adds,

**Your doodle has given me another idea, Tom. I'll talk to you later.**

OK, sir

I wonder what that's about?

After school, I meet Derek outside the hall so we can check out and swap books together.

I'm HOPING that maybe I might find a copy of **ALIEN SCALE MONSTERS - IN SPACE.**

The hall quickly fills up. It's very busy and Derek's already found some good books.

My dad will like this one.

I'm showing Florence my alien monster books when she tells me,

"There's a kid over there who's got an alien monster book to swap."

HE DOES?

GREAT! I SQUEEZE my way through the crowd until I find him... There he is, HOLDING  a copy of ...

☾ ... **ALIEN SCALE MONSTER is HERE.** Oh.

AND it looks like MY old copy as well.

"I swapped it with THAT boy over there," he says.

THAT BOY - is  Marcus Meldrew. Who else.

He's already reading **Alien Scale Monsters – In Space.**

Oh well, he'll never swap it with me.

    Never mind. I spot a book that Granny Mavis might like instead.

 (You never know, she might even use it.)

When I get home, Mum, Dad and  are having some tea, which is handy. I show Mum the books that I swapped and give Granny Mavis her cookbook.

She says, "HOW lovely! I'll definitely use this one." (She won't.)

 Granddad Bob says, "We popped round because we have something to give you too, Tom." Which, along with the CAKE, is a VERY nice surprise. (Especially after I picked off the whole pea pods that were on top.)

Whole pea pods

Granny hands me a bag and inside there is ... let me see ...

(I can use my BOOK TOKEN PRIZE to
buy something ELSE now - RESULT!)

I think that THIS has actually
been

# MY
# BEST
# BOOK
# WEEK
# EVER!

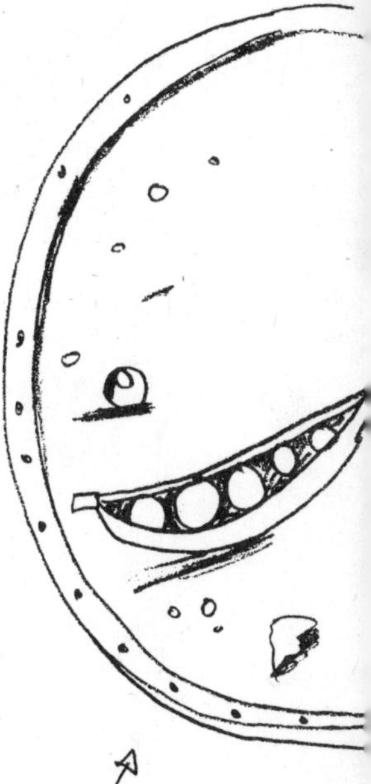

Granny's pea
Pod cake

(So far.)

The end.

**MORE GOOD NEWS!!**
Mr Fullerman was SO impressed with my doodle drawing in the book (that was an accident), he wants me to DESIGN a special BOOK PLATE STICKER* for the school to use. How good is THAT!

Here it is.

This Book belongs TO

Oakfield School (hands off)

*A book plate is a fancy sticker that goes into a book with someone's name on it.

This is MY book

I did a few more.

This book belongs to

Which book will
you choose?